MIXED ME!

by
TAYE DIGGS

Illustrated by
SHANE W. EVANS

SQUARE FISH
FEIWEL AND FRIENDS
NEW YORK

HEY, now!
They call me Mixed-up Mike.
My hair is like **WOW!**
Super-crazy-fresh-cool, man.
YEAH!

I like to go **FAST**!
No one can stop me
as the wind combs through
my zigzag curly 'do!

"What's happenin', Captain?" my daddy says.
"HI!" I say.
"BYE!" I say.

"Hey, sweet boy, sweet pie, honey boo,"
my mom coos.
She's my one and only, never lonely.

"HI!" I say.
"BYE!" I say.

Sometimes when we're together
people stare at whatever.

"Your mom and dad don't match,"
they say, and scratch their heads.

See, my dad's a deep brown and
my mom's rich cream and honey.
Then people see me, and they look at us funny.

My mom and dad say I'm a blend
of dark and light.
"We mixed you perfectly,
and got you JUST RIGHT!"

There are so many flavors
to savor and taste!
Why pick only one
color or face?
Why pick one race?

Some kids at school want me to choose
who I cruise with.
I'm down for **FUN** with everyone.

Why pick one race?

I'm a combo plate!
Garden salad, rice and beans—
tasting GREAT!
But wait!

And if they care too much
about my hair too much
that it's not straight enough,
I say, "It's MY HAIR,
don't touch!"

I'm doing my thing, so don't forget it.

If you don't get it, then you don't get it.

UH-HUH, I said it!

I'm a beautiful blend of dark and light,
I was mixed up perfectly,
and I'm JUST RIGHT!

They call me Mixed-up Mike,
but that name should be fixed.
I'm not mixed up,
I just happen to be mixed.

I dedicate this book to Walker, Shane, Olu, Kasey,
Thembi, Amanza, Braker, Noah, and all the crazy-coifed,
buttery-skinned, individual mixties of the world.
Thank y'all for being you and helping me better accept myself.
—T.D.

Thank God for the gift.
Dedicated to my Mother Marie and Father Jackie Vance.
—S.W.E.

SQUARE
FISH

An imprint of Macmillan Publishing Group, LLC
120 Broadway, New York, NY 10271
mackids.com

Our books may be purchased in bulk for promotional, educational, or business use.
Please contact your local bookseller or the Macmillan Corporate and
Premium Sales Department at (800) 221-7945 ext. 5442 or
by email at MacmillanSpecialMarkets@macmillan.com.

Library of Congress Cataloging-in-Publication Data Available

ISBN 978-1-250-76985-5 (paperback)
ISBN 978-1-250-09974-7 (ebook)

Originally published in the United States by Feiwel and Friends
First Square Fish edition, 2021
Book designed by Kathleen Breitenfeld and Rich Deas
Square Fish logo designed by Filomena Tuosto

1 3 5 7 9 10 8 6 4 2

AR: 1.8 / LEXILE: AD540L